Run, Friend, Run!

Joseph Coelho

Illustrated by **Davide Ortu**

OXFORD
UNIVERSITY PRESS

I am a children's author and poet. My first book to ever get published was called *Werewolf Club Rules*, a poetry collection that won the CLPE Poetry Award (CliPPA). I like writing for many ages. I've also written a little bit for TV.

When I'm not writing, I like to run. I have completed the Brighton and London Marathons and hope to run a few more yet. *Run, Friend, Run!* was inspired by a cross-country run that I did at school which I completed in the rain, arm-in-arm with my friend.

Joseph Coelho

Chapter 1
The Runner

The evil Dorg horde was upon them, shooting slime from their tentacles and gurgling their monstrous roars.

Ben's avatar found a health pack next to a pile of steaming Dorg gunk when he noticed that David was on his last energy bar.

'David! Quick! Come to me, I've got a
health pack!' David's avatar limped over just
in time to load back up to full health before
the Dorg horde attacked them again.

'It's Dorg zapping time!' cried Ben and
David as they charged up their zappers and
turned the Dorg horde into a puddle of slime.

'That was amazing!' said Ben. 'We've never
got that far before.'

'Thanks for the health pack! You saved me
from becoming Dorg dinner,' said David.

'Right, you two – that's enough gaming. Go out and get some fresh air.' Ben's mum started ushering them out of the room.

'But Mum, we've nearly completed *Attack of the Dorg Horde*!'

'I don't care. You are not spending all day on that machine. Take your scooter out. And besides, David's dad just called to say he needs to get home for tea. You can scoot to David's and back to get some exercise.'

'OK,' the boys reluctantly agreed, and headed downstairs to collect their scooters.

Ben clipped on his red helmet. He had painted it to look like his avatar's. In the real world he was Ben St. Clair. In *Attack of the Dorg Horde* he was Dillon Wild-Ranch: Commander of the Dorg Zapping Alliance! David's helmet was covered in bug stickers.

'Where did you get those stickers from?' asked Ben.

'From my *Bugs Monthly* magazine,' explained David. 'Each month you find out more about bugs and sometimes there's a free gift. I have more at home – I'll bring some into school tomorrow.'

Ben lived at the top of Dukesbury Park Road and David lived at the bottom. In-between their houses was Dukesbury Park. The park was on a steep hill, and Ben and David loved racing up and down on their scooters almost as much as they loved playing *Attack of the Dorg Horde*. It was midsummer and the sun was shining brightly as they sped down the hill, getting faster and faster as they went.

'I'm as fast as the giant house spider. That's the fastest spider in the world!' shouted David.

'I'm as fast as Dorg slime!' shouted Ben.

And that's when they saw her. The runner. A woman in black sports gear with her hair in a bun, running towards them, attacking the hill at speed. She was running faster than Dorg slime, faster than house spiders, faster than their scooters, and finally she disappeared up the hill behind them.

'Wow, that woman was so fast!' gasped Ben.

They stopped their scooters and watched in awe as the woman became a speck in the distance. The boys were amazed – she looked as if she could do or be anything she wanted.

'If I could run as fast as that I would enter the Olympics for sure,' said Ben.

'I would go to Peru and chase down giant spiders,' said David.

'How much training do you think it takes to get that fast?'

'It must take ages. Melvin Mandible, one of the experts from *Bugs Monthly*, said he trained for five years to become an entomologist.'

'What's that?' asked Ben.

'An insect specialist.'

'Yeah, but that's brain stuff, like studying. I'm talking about training your body to be fast and strong, like that runner. She was superhero-fast! That must take forever.'

'Yeah, she must have started running when she was a baby,' said David.

'I bet she could run before she could walk.'

'I bet she was born with trainers on.'

'I bet she was so fast her pram had a speed limit!' Ben exclaimed.

They both burst out laughing. 'I'd better get home for dinner,' said David, 'but let's ask Mr Ele about running in our sports lesson tomorrow. He knows all about that stuff.'

As David headed home, Ben scooted slowly back up the hill, his head full of ideas about running fast, *super-fast* towards his dreams.

Chapter 2
A Training Schedule

'Here are the spider stickers,' said David as they got to school the following day. He handed over a couple of brilliantly lifelike spider stickers: one of a huge black and orange tarantula, and the other of a camel spider.

'The camel spiders are mean-looking, a lot like the Rantokors in this game,' said Ben, pulling out the latest copy of *Game Pizazz* magazine. 'Mum said I can download it tonight. Do you want to come round and play?'

'Do you get to play as the spider thingies?'
'The Rantokors ... yes,' replied Ben.
'Yes, yes, yes!' cheered David.
'I knew you'd love the chance to play as a spider, even if it is a giant alien spider from the Arachna dimension!' Ben and David exchanged grins and a high five before heading into their classroom.

Later that morning, their sports lesson began. 'Collect a bib. It's yellows against reds,' said Mr Ele as the class prepared for a game of baseball. Ben didn't normally like sports but today was different. He had been inspired. He couldn't stop thinking about the runner they had seen running up the hill in the park yesterday. When it was his turn to bat, he found an excitement tingling in his belly as he imagined running as fast as she had.

When Ben stepped up to the batting area there was an audible groan from some of the other kids on the pitch, especially Trevor Snorton. Ben lifted his bat to hit the ball.

'Try to hit it at least once, *Benjiiiii*,' Trevor teased.

'You can do it, Ben!' shouted David, even though he was on the opposing team. Leila Jayatissa was pitching. She had a hard throw that everyone was a little scared of. (Ola Adayemi was hit by one of her pitches last year and rushed to the nurse with a bleeding nose!) Leila raised her arm ready to bowl. Ben lifted the bat ... and what happened next was a blur.

Ben wasn't even thinking about hitting the ball – he was thinking more about running, about the thrill of running around the pitch, getting faster and faster, running like his super-powered avatar Dillion Wild-Ranch. Then the ball was coming straight at him, straight at his nose! And WHACK! He somehow hit it, and not just a little hit, it was a big hit, a huge hit, a hit that had the ball sailing so high that the whole class was squinting up into the sky.

'Run, Ben! *Run*!' came David's yell.

Adrenaline flooded Ben's body as he dropped the bat and ran past first base. Out of the corner of his eye, he spotted a group of yellow bibs sprinting towards the bushes on the far side of the pitch where the ball had landed. He was approaching second base and could feel his legs pumping effortlessly beneath him. A smile crept onto his face.

How fast can I go? he wondered, as second base passed underfoot. He was dimly aware of the yellow bibs now deep in the bushes and Trevor shouting insults at his teammates. Ben's legs were a blur and his lungs were aching, but he wanted to go faster, to be as fast as the runner in the park. Third base was coming up when he heard *'Got it!'* coming from Trevor. Trevor hurled the ball in Ben's direction. Ben tried to put on a burst of speed, but his legs refused to go any faster and his lungs were straining.

'You can do it!' shouted David.

'David, help *your* team!' replied Mr Ele as the ball sailed past David, who was too busy watching Ben run to catch it.

Ben ran on past third base even though his legs were like jelly, and then he heard it: '*Out*!'

Tariq had swiped the ball and managed to stop Ben's home run. Ben collapsed onto the floor, laughing.

'Why are you laughing? You lost,' scowled Trevor. Ben and David just looked at each other and laughed even harder. Inspired by Ben's rush of sporting energy, they both felt the tingle of possibility of becoming super-speedy runners.

* * *

At the end of lesson Mr Ele took Ben and David aside.

'I was really impressed with you two today. I've never seen you so committed, Ben, and David – the support you were giving him was brilliant. Granted, it was for the wrong team, but that was very sporting of you. I hope to see more of that from both of you.'

Mr Ele turned to pick up the box of bibs as Ben nudged David in the ribs.

'Actually, we wanted to ask you about training to become proper runners,' said David.

'OK,' said Mr Ele, 'what did you want to know?'

'Well,' continued David, 'we saw this woman running in the park yesterday and she was fast and strong. She looked like she could do anything! We were wondering how people become as great as her?'

'Well, it's important to eat healthily and to train regularly,' explained Mr Ele.

'Oh, how long does that take?' asked Ben.

'It's a gradual process, but if you start running once or twice a week you should feel the difference fairly quickly.'

'Will we get faster and stronger?' asked David. 'And be able to run for long distances?'

'Definitely, if you keep the training up. A good way to train is to have something to aim for, and ... actually, you're in luck. It's the annual School Park Run soon. If you two are serious, I can speak to your parents and draw up a four-week training timetable, but it will mean running twice a week – maybe more if you can manage it.'

'And we'll get as fast as the runner in the park?' asked David.

'That's up to you. The more you train, the faster you'll get, but good runners need to build up their stamina, too. It won't be easy and you'll need to be committed.'

'Can we start today?' Ben asked.

Mr Ele laughed his big, friendly laugh.
'I'll make a training schedule for you later
today and we'll have a chat with your parents.'

Chapter 3
A Hurdle

As the bell rang for the end of school, Ben and David found Mr Ele speaking to Ben's mum in the playground.

'I've just been talking to your mum about your interest in running, Ben,' Mr Ele explained.

'I'll train with you, boys, if you don't mind – I want to get back into running and I can keep you both on track with Mr Ele's schedule,' said Ben's mum.

'That would be amazing!' said both boys at once. 'You can time us.'

'Absolutely!' said Ben's mum with a smile.

'That's settled then,' said Mr Ele. 'Here's a training schedule for you both. Remember to eat well and get plenty of sleep, too.'

The boys nodded seriously, then set off for home feeling giddy with excitement.

* * *

Mr Ele's training schedule was brilliant. It had two thirty-minute runs a week, with an optional third run on the weekend.

'Let's do these runs every day,' suggested David.

'Definitely,' agreed Ben.

They ran ahead of Ben's mum on the way home. Every now and then they took another peek at the schedule.

'Let's sprint to the next bus stop,' challenged David, so they did.

'Let's do lunges to Grafton Road,' said Ben as he took a wide step and lunged down. David laughed but joined in all the same. It took them longer to move in this way, but they kept going until they lunged passed Trevor Snorton, who couldn't resist teasing them.

'Er, what are you fools doing?' sniggered his voice from behind them.

Trevor started dancing around them. 'You look so pathetic. What are you doing that for?'

'We're training,' said Ben.

'For what?'

'The School Park Run,' said David.

'No one trains for that – it's easy.'

'Well, we're going to train so we can be the fastest runners there,' said David.

Trevor snorted with laughter and Ben could feel his temper rising. His mum always said to just take a deep breath and walk away from trouble, but some people made it so hard. The boys continued to lunge in silence and soon Trevor got bored. But, before Trevor sped off down the road on his black trick scooter, he made one final comment.

'You can't both be the fastest. One of you will always be faster than the other, but it won't matter 'cos you're both losers.'

* * *

Ben and David lost their enthusiasm for lunging after that. It felt like their tingle of excitement had been smudged out by Trevor's teasing. The whole idea of running had lost its gleam, and the question neither of them wanted to ask hung like a cloud in the air.

'Who do you think will be fastest?' asked Ben eventually as they rounded the corner on to their street.

'I don't care what Trevor says' replied David. 'If we train together like we've planned, then we'll both be equally fast and really strong; if we can do that, we can do anything.'

Ben let out a sigh of relief. 'I think so, too', he said as he turned for home.

Later that week, the boys were back in the park, with Ben's mum agreeing to watch and time them.

'OK, the training schedule says that we should do a gentle run to start with. Sounds straightforward,' said Ben. 'Let's do this.'

* * *

The sun was shining lazily in the sky, and Ben felt special as he and David started to jog around the park's perimeter path. He felt like they belonged with the runners!

They were running in unison to start off with but then David pulled a little ahead.

'Hey, not too fast,' puffed Ben. 'The schedule says to start slow.'

They found a pace that suited them both for a while, but then Ben got a bit quicker, then David increased his speed. Then Ben sped up, then David revved up and then suddenly without warning, they were both trying to outdo each other. And that's when they saw her again: the super-fast woman running in her black sports gear. She zoomed past the boys and they immediately accelerated in an attempt to catch her. Ben's breath was rasping in his throat, his heart became a drum in his chest beating louder and louder, urging him forward. All that mattered was catching up with the woman, to be as strong as her, as quick as her, to prove he could do anything, to show the world he was the fastest runner.

The path curved around Dukesbury duck-pond. Up ahead a dog walker struggled with a tangle of dogs. But the runner weaved effortlessly past them. Ben and David weren't so agile. David barged into Ben to avoid a playful Labrador. Ben took a stumbling dive into the duck-pond with an almighty quacking splash!

David staggered to a stop and turned to help his friend, but it was too late. Ben was sodden and soaked in the pond, with ducks and geese swimming noisily away.

'I'm sorry! It was the dogs and the leads ... ' gasped David.

'You were just trying to be faster than me,' spluttered Ben.

'No ... I mean ... yes ... I mean, I was trying to catch up with the woman. You were racing me, too!'

'No, I said we had to take it nice and easy.'

'Yeah, but then you started racing,' argued David.

'Only because you were racing!' protested Ben.

'But I was racing because you were racing!'

'Well, friends don't race and if being the fastest is that important to you then you should train by yourself!' As soon as Ben said the words, he wished he hadn't, but he was wet, people were laughing at him and he was fed up. He could already see his mum running to them from her bench.

'Fine,' said David. He turned around and stormed home, leaving Ben alone and wet in the pond.

Chapter 4
Back Over Old Ground

After the incident in the park, Ben and David didn't speak to each other for weeks. School felt cold and frosty as they avoided each other in the corridors and worked in silence during lessons. To make things worse, Trevor's teasing became relentless.

'What's wrong with you two, why aren't you talking?'

The boys ignored him as much as they could but when Trevor tripped while trying to push into the lunch queue, they almost shared a laugh. But then the memory of the racing and the pond came flooding back. Ben couldn't believe that David would try to go faster than him when they had agreed to run together. There was a niggling part of his mind that kept saying: *you were racing too*. But then he remembered the shove, and how it felt to sit in the pond with people laughing at him. The silence continued.

Training without David wasn't as fun, but Ben's parents had helped. They took turns to run with Ben, which was actually pretty cool. Mum had found her old marathon-finisher T-shirt from years ago. It was Ben's size and still in great condition, so he started wearing it, convinced that it would impart some extra running power. Mum had shown him how to steady his pace, which basically meant not running too fast at the start so that he had enough energy to complete the whole distance of the run.

When Ben ran with his dad, they would practise sprints, and sometimes all three would run together.

On the last weekend before the School Park Run, Ben and his mum did one last training run. Dad unfolded the graph he'd been keeping of all Ben's running times. Just like Mr Ele had said, he'd got quicker during his training, except for one of the weekend runs when he had stayed up too late playing a new computer game the night before. Today, Ben hoped to break his record. He was proud of his progress, and one day secretly hoped to be as fast as the runner in the park.

The run started easily enough. They headed down the hill past the pond and the flower beds and then back up the hill and through the trees to do it all again. Ben's legs felt strong ... he was a runner now. It was on the second lap that he felt his stomach lurch.

'Isn't that David?' said his mum, as David ran up the path behind them with his older sister. Ben immediately sped up and fixed his gaze straight ahead so that he wouldn't have to look David in the eyes. They ran the entire circuit without so much as a nod. It felt horrible.

* * *

When the run was finished and his new time recorded, Ben wasn't smiling. He had beaten his own record, but it didn't feel that great without his best friend to share it with.

Ben's parents sat him down on a bench in the sun.

'What was all that about? You two used to be so close,' said Dad.

'Yeah, well that was before he pushed me in the pond,' said Ben.

'Oh, Ben, I'm sure he didn't mean to. He did say it was an accident,' replied Mum.

'It didn't feel like an accident.' Although deep down Ben wasn't sure that was true.

'Friends often don't get along,' said Dad. 'But what makes a friendship really special, really deep, is how we stay friends even after we fall out.'

'I bet you miss having someone to play your games with ... ' smiled Mum.

'Or to tell you about Marvin Mandible's latest insect discoveries,' continued Dad.

'I don't care,' Ben grumbled. But inside his belly he could tell he was lying. He did care, and he did miss David and his insect facts. Running with his parents had been fun but sometimes he wanted to run with his friend. But too much time had passed now. They hadn't spoken for so long it seemed impossible that they could ever be friends again.

Chapter 5
The Run

It was the day of the School Park Run and the sky was grey.

'I can't believe how miserable it is,' complained Leila to Ben as the class trekked to Dukesbury Park to do the run.

'Line up behind your class, please!' Mr Ele shouted, hustling the stragglers along.

'Now, listen carefully,' said Mr Ele. 'There are clear signs along the whole route and Ms Chatterjee, Mr Stanton, Ms Irwin and Mr Nowak are standing at each turning, so there really is no excuse for going the wrong way. You are expected to run the whole way, but if for any reason you need to stop, then follow the route back to the nearest teacher.'

'What if I get tired, Sir?' asked Ola.

'If you get tired you can slow down,' replied Mr Ele.

'What if I want to walk?' asked Tariq.

'Walk if you must, but this is a running challenge, so we expect you all to give it a good go,' said Mr Ele encouragingly. 'And remember, there are prizes for first, second and third place, but also special prizes for those we see putting real effort into their run and showing real determination. It's not just about being the fastest; it's about continuing when the going gets tough.'

They were led to the starting line: a red ribbon strung between two massive trees. It was weird seeing all the other classes outside in the park with its trees, bushes and dog walkers. Ben could see David further down the starting line wearing a T-shirt with a huge house spider on it.

'I'm going to beat you even though I've done no training and you've done loads,' came Trevor's slimy hiss in Ben's ear. Ben ignored him. He had to focus.

'When I blow the whistle, you can begin!' shouted Mr Ele. 'Three, two, one ... '

The whistle came loud and clear through the grey, humid air. All of the classes surged forward in an excited gaggle, but not Ben. He started slow and steady, breathing in time and watching where he was putting his feet. He liked this feeling he got when running, a feeling of being alive and strong.

I'll take it easy for the first half like Mum said, and then for the second half, I'll speed up. Maybe I'll even sail past Trevor, thought Ben as more and more pupils streamed past him. The first part of the route was fairly flat but then it started to slowly angle uphill through the park's tall trees. It was here that Ben's steady pace served him well as he started passing his classmates who were now slowing down. He could see David just ahead of him. He was doing well too, attacking the hill and looking strong – just like the runner in the park – and then the rain started to fall.

It was just a few drops at first but then the skies opened up and the summer rain plummeted down. It was warm, wet and heavy, and before long everyone was soaked. Ben dug in, keeping his pace steady and strong.

'Give me some of that marathon power,' he whispered to his mum's old T-shirt. He couldn't believe his mum had once run the full twenty-six miles of a marathon in it! The route started to angle downhill and now the path was really muddy, and puddles had started to form.

Ben passed Ms Irwin as she called out to everyone, 'You're halfway! Keep going! Well done!'

Halfway! Ben dug in and started going quicker. He couldn't see David who was clearly running faster than him, but that didn't matter now. He just had to get to the end and hopefully beat his previous best time. That was what really mattered: the progress he could make on each run. Ben turned a corner and spotted David's spider T-shirt. Ben resisted the urge to race forward – it was important to keep to your pace. He felt proud that his friend (ex-friend, he reminded himself) was running so well. And that's when David tripped.

It happened in a flash. David's foot landed in a puddle and he crashed to the ground. It seemed as if the rain started to fall even harder. Without hesitation, Ben sped towards him, not caring about his pace. David had fallen, and Ben had to go and help his friend.

'David, are you OK?'

David looked up sheepishly. 'I think I've twisted my ankle.'

Ben helped David up. 'Does it hurt when you stand on it?'

57

'Only a little. I think I'll be OK – I'll just go a bit slower. But you should get going, run your fastest time.'

Ben thought for a moment about the excitement they had both felt at seeing the woman in the park, how much fun it had been to run with his friend, and how sad he had felt when they weren't talking.

'Nah, that's OK,' he replied. 'Let's finish this run together.'

Ben linked arms with David, and they started to run. They were clumsy at first, but after a while they found a rhythm and even overtook some of the other students, including Trevor who was panting and soaked. The rain fell harder, but they didn't mind. They kept on together, keeping pace together, crossing the finishing line together.

Ben and David collapsed in a wet heap on the floor as the other students gave them a massive round of applause.

'That was great!' gasped Ben.

'Thanks for helping me,' puffed David.

'I'm sorry about all the stupid not speaking stuff,' said Ben.

'Me, too,' said David.

And just as he spoke, the rain stopped.

'If we had waited an hour, we would have missed the rain entirely,' complained Leila as the sun peeped down on Ben and David's renewed friendship.

* * *

The following day in assembly Mr Ele called out the winners of the School Park Run. Ben and David were shocked when their names were called out – not for being first, or second or even third, but because they had shown true character in crossing the finishing line together.

Ben and David both blushed as Mr Ele announced, 'These two have shown us all that any race is much easier, much more fun and creates much more of a memory when we choose to run together.'

As Ben and David returned to their seats clutching their medals, Ben felt something settle into place inside him – a strength and a confidence that weren't there before. It was a feeling that tingled when he thought about running. But especially when he thought about running with his friend.